JULIUS CAESAR

JULIUS CAESAR

Retold by Tony Bradman

Illustrated by Mark Oldroyd

A & C Black • London

First published 2011 by
A & C Black Publishers Ltd
36 Soho Square, London, W1D 3QY

www.acblack.com

ISBN 978-1-4081-1154-3

A CIP catalogue for this book is available from the British Library.

This book is produced using paper that is made from wood grown
in managed, sustainable forests. It is natural, renewable and
recyclable. The logging and manufacturing processes conform
to the environmental regulations of the country of origin.

Printed and bound in Great Britain
by CPI Cox & Wyman, Reading, RG1 8EX.

CONTENTS

List of characters

Julius Caesar, *Roman statesman and general*

Octavius, *Triumvir after Caesar's death*

Mark Antony, *friend of Caesar and a Triumvir*

Lepidus, *third member of the Triumvirate*

Marcus Brutus, *leader of conspiracy against Caesar*

Cassius, *instigator of conspiracy against Caesar*

Casca, *conspirator*

Trebonius, *conspirator*

Caius Ligarius, *conspirator*

Decius Brutus, *conspirator*

Metellus Cimber, *conspirator*

Cinna, *conspirator*

Calpurnia, *wife of Caesar*

Portia, *wife of Brutus*

Popilius Lena, *senator*

Cicero, *senator*

Flavius, *tribune*

Marullus, *tribune*

Lucilius, *supporter of Brutus*

Titinius, *supporter of Brutus*

Messala, *supporter of Brutus*

Volumnius, *supporter of Brutus*

Clitus, *servant to Brutus*

Strato, *servant to Brutus*

Lucius, *servant to Brutus*

Dardanius, *servant to Brutus*

Pindarus, *servant to Cassius*

A soothsayer

The ghost of Caesar

Act One
The Eagle
Soars

The people of Rome laughed and sang as they crowded through the streets of the city. It was March, the month when the Festival of Lupercal was held to mark the beginning of spring, always a good excuse to have fun. But something else had helped to make the people even happier. The war between Rome's great men for control of the ancient city and its growing empire had just ended, leaving a single winner, the mighty Julius Caesar. And now he had returned to celebrate his victory with feasts and special games laid on for the masses.

Not everyone was cheerful, though. Two nobles stood at the side of a street, their long white togas bright in the gloom of an overcast day, their faces hard and bitter as they watched the crowds enjoying themselves. Flavius and Marullus were supporters of Pompey, the general who had been Caesar's enemy in the war. But Pompey was dead, and Caesar had no more rivals.

At last, Flavius could stand it no more. He stepped out in front of a group of labourers who were chanting 'CAESAR! CAESAR!' as they strolled along.

'What are you doing?' said Flavius. 'Have you no shame?'

'None at all!' they grinned. 'We're going to see the mighty Caesar!'

'Have you forgotten Pompey already?' snarled Marullus. 'There was a time when you would have waited all day just for a glimpse of him. Now you put on your best clothes and cheer the man responsible for his death! Be gone, and pray the Gods don't punish you for being so cruel and hard-hearted.'

The labourers simply laughed and jeered, and Flavius drew his friend away into the shadows. 'Let's tear down the decorations that have been put up to honour Caesar,' Flavius whispered. 'He thinks he can soar above us like an eagle, but he'll fly a little lower once we've plucked some feathers from his wings...'

They hurried off, and soon Caesar himself came into the same street. At first glance he was much like any other balding Roman noble – he certainly wasn't tall or handsome. But look more closely and you could see the strength in his face, the steely determination to get whatever he wanted, the aura of power.

He was accompanied by his wife Calpurnia, his second-in-command Mark Antony, and several others – important Romans such as Brutus and his wife Portia, the great orator Cicero, the senators Cassius and Casca. Behind them all was a large crowd of people jostling each other and yelling Caesar's name.

One voice was much louder than the rest, and caught the general's attention.

'Who calls to me?' he said. 'What do you want? Caesar will listen!'

Caesar often spoke in this way, using his name to refer to himself rather than saying 'I' or 'me'. Some thought it was to show that he was better than other men, while some even suspected he did it to make himself sound like a god.

'Do as he says, whoever you are!' Mark Antony roared. 'Caesar must be obeyed!' Caesar's second-in-command was a solid, muscular man, a soldier from head to foot. But there was a spark of passion in his face, too.

An old man stepped forward. He had a mop of wild white hair and wore a long, ragged robe. 'Beware the Ides of March!' he hissed, his eyes rolling.

The Romans had special names for some dates – the 15th day of March was always called the 'Ides'.

'What is he talking about?' said Caesar.

'Tomorrow will be the Ides of March,' murmured Brutus, a man with a dark, brooding face. His toga was made of the finest wool, and so white it seemed to gleam. 'He must be a soothsayer,' Brutus continued. 'I think he's giving you a warning of some kind.'

'Well, he's obviously mad then, a dreamer,'

said Caesar, laughing and confident. 'Tomorrow has no fears for Caesar. This way, everyone...'

Caesar moved on, heading for the Forum, the great open space that had always been the heart of the ancient city. Most of the crowd followed him, but Brutus didn't, staying behind instead, his face thoughtful. Cassius saw him stop, and hung back, too. They ended up standing together by one of Rome's many temples to the gods, its tall white columns rising high above them.

'Aren't you going to watch any more of the fun, Brutus?' said Cassius. He was thin and bony and had the face of a hawk, his nose like a sharp beak.

'No, I'm not interested,' said Brutus. 'Don't let me stop you, though.'

He turned to leave, but Cassius held his arm. 'Wait, Brutus,' he said. 'I've wanted to speak to you for a while. You've seemed rather ... *distant* recently.'

'I'm sorry, Cassius,' said Brutus, sighing.

'It's just that I've had a lot on my mind. But don't worry, I still think of you as a friend.'

'That's good, because what I have to say is very important,' Cassius said quietly, glancing over his shoulder to make sure nobody could overhear their conversation. 'Many of the best men in Rome have enormous respect for your judgement, Brutus, and wish you could see the truth of what's going on.'

'Are you leading me into danger, Cassius?' Brutus said, glancing over his shoulder, too. 'Perhaps my judgement isn't as good as you think.'

'You're too modest, Brutus,' said Cassius. 'And you know me too well to think I'm trying to trick you. I don't flatter men to gain their confidence then betray them afterwards to all and sundry. Now that *would* be dangerous…'

Suddenly, there was a clamour of people cheering in the distance. Brutus and Cassius exchanged a look, but they both knew the noise came from the Forum.

'What does that shouting mean?' Brutus murmured, gripping Cassius by the arm himself now. 'I fear the people may have chosen Caesar as their king.'

'Oh, so you *fear* such a thing, do you?' said Cassius, his eyes glittering, a smile on his lips. 'Then I'm guessing that you don't want it to happen.'

'I don't, even though Caesar and I have always been friends,' said Brutus, his face clouded, his eyes downcast. Then he looked up and frowned. 'Just what are you getting at, Cassius?' he said impatiently. 'Come on, out with it.'

'Very well,' said Cassius, shrugging. 'It's simple. I'm tired of being made to live in awe of somebody who is no better than me. I was born just as free as Caesar, and so were you, Brutus. Did you know he once challenged me to a swimming race across the River Tiber, and would have drowned if I hadn't saved him? I saw him shaking with cold and fear, and I heard him whining like a sick girl. I can't believe the same man now lords it over the rest of us.'

There was another burst of shouting in the Forum, much louder this time. 'It seems even more honours are being heaped on Caesar,' Brutus muttered.

'Why, he strides over our little world like a giant, while we tiny men dodge his huge feet,' said Cassius with a sour laugh. 'But *we* should be masters of our fates. It's our own fault if we allow ourselves to be ruled. Your name is as good as Caesar's, so why should his be spoken more? When has Rome been a city big enough for only one man? Was there not another Brutus in the past, a great ancestor of yours, who rose up against a tyrant king? I think there was...'

Once Rome had been ruled by kings, but the people had thrown them out. Since then it had been a Republic governed by the Senate, a body of men who debated important issues and appointed the chief officers of the state. The senators were mostly rich, older men, but they considered each other as equals. At least they had until recent years. But then individuals like Pompey and Caesar had begun to grow in power and influence – something Brutus didn't like at all.

'Enough, Cassius,' said Brutus. 'I'll consider what you've said, and I'll let you know what I think in due course. Although you should know this – I would rather leave Rome forever than live under a tyrant. Wait, here comes Caesar again....' The crowd had returned, filling the street once more. 'Something must have happened,' said Brutus. 'He is upset, and the others look shocked.'

'Yes, you're right,' said Cassius, his expression one of cold calculation. 'Let's grab Casca as he goes past. He'll tell us what's been going on.'

The two men retreated further behind the temple's columns and waited for their chance. But Caesar had seen them, and turned to Mark Antony. 'That Cassius has a lean and hungry look,' he said, his eyes narrowed and suspicious, and his face as pale as a corpse's. 'He thinks too much. Such men can be very dangerous.'

'Oh, he's not someone you should fear, Caesar,' said Mark Antony.

'Caesar fears no one, but men like Cassius are always jealous of those who are greater. Come, tell me everything you know about him...'

Brutus and Cassius had heard nothing of this, intent as they were on catching Casca. Cassius tugged Casca's cloak and pulled him into the shadows behind the columns. The crowd flowed on, everyone's eyes still focused on Caesar.

'What has happened, Casca?' said Brutus. 'Why is Caesar so moved?'

'He was offered a crown, that's all,' said Casca. 'And he turned it down.'

'Good,' snapped Brutus. 'But why did the crowd raise another clamour?'

'Because Caesar was offered the crown *again*,' said Casca, with a snort. 'In fact, he was offered the crown three times. I've never seen anything like it.'

'None of us have,' said Cassius, glancing at Brutus. 'Who offered it to him?'

'Why, Mark Antony, of course,' said Casca. 'But I think it was all just play-acting. Each time Mark Antony offered Caesar the crown, Caesar made a big show of waving it away, although the last time he let his eyes linger on it for quite a while. The crowd thought this was all wonderful, of course, and might even have made him accept the crown in the end. But then Caesar fainted.'

'What do you mean, he fainted?' said Cassius, surprise in his voice.

'He fell down and foamed at the mouth, and couldn't speak,' said Casca.

'*That* wasn't play-acting,' said Brutus. 'Few people know it, but Caesar has the falling sickness, and often has fits. What did he say when he recovered?'

'Only that his illness was to blame if he had

done or said anything wrong,' said Casca, shrugging. 'And he asked everyone to forgive him. Which they did, of course. There is some other news, though. Flavius and Marullus have been arrested for taking down the decorations that were put up to honour Caesar…'

The men talked for a while longer, but at last they said their farewells. Brutus went home, and Casca to dinner with some friends, leaving Cassius alone by the temple. It was almost evening and the sky had clouded over, but Cassius barely noticed. He was thinking about his conversation with Brutus, and working out what to do next. Cassius had long known that Caesar was suspicious of him, and also that Brutus and Caesar were friends. But now it was clear that Brutus wasn't happy with the way things were going. Cassius smiled. A little more effort and Brutus would be on the right side, no doubt about it. 'Caesar might think he's safe now,' Cassius murmured. 'But we'll shake him before we're done.'

Cassius strode off. There were people he had to see, plotting to be done.

Thunder boomed and lightning flashed as darkness fell, chasing the tired crowds from the streets. Strange things were seen, too – fire dropping from the sky, a slave holding up a hand that seemed to burn like twenty torches but left the man's skin unharmed. And on his way home later that night, Casca met a lion by the Capitol, the building where the Senate met. It stared at him, then walked on by.

Later, Casca bumped into Cassius in a dark street, and told him all about it.

'What a dreadful night!' he said. A cold breeze swept around them, and Casca shivered. 'It's almost as if the gods are trying to tell us something.'

'They're warning us, Casca,' said Cassius. 'I could name a certain man who is like this dreadful night, a man who has become dangerous and difficult...'

'You mean Caesar, don't you?' murmured

Casca. Thunder cracked above them as if to answer his question, and a spear of lightning split the sky. 'I heard at dinner that he is going to the Senate tomorrow to be made our king.'

'I'll need to wear my dagger then,' said Cassius. 'Caesar is a wolf, and that's because he thinks we Romans are sheep. But at least some of us are going to do something about it. Give me your hand if you're willing to join us.'

'Gladly,' said Casca, and they shook hands. 'But what about Brutus? Our cause would be much stronger if such a respected man were on our side.'

'Don't worry,' said Cassius. 'He's three quarters persuaded already. But come, it's past midnight. Let's meet again before sunrise, at Brutus' house.'

They parted once more and went their separate ways, knowing that tomorrow would be the most fateful of days.

Act Two
Strange Dreams

Brutus paced up and down in his garden, unable to sleep, his mind racing, a couple of small oil lamps casting a fitful glow and keeping the shadows at bay. He went over his conversation with Cassius again and again, teasing out all its hidden meanings and implications. Although the truth was he'd been thinking the same thing as Cassius for some time. Caesar was a huge problem for the Republic, and something would have to be done about him. But what?

'He must die,' Brutus said quietly to himself at last. He stood still, holding that thought for a moment. He had nothing personal against Caesar. Anything he and Cassius did would be for the good of Rome. But how could they justify such an act to the people? The masses loved Caesar, and up until now they had no reason to complain. He had been very careful not to play the tyrant to them.

But of course all that might change if Caesar became their king. Men often put on a show of being meek and mild as they climbed the ladder of ambition. Then, once they reached the top, they revealed their true selves. They had to stop that happening with Caesar. They would tell the people he was a baby serpent in its egg, waiting to hatch into a monster. Far better to kill him now while still in the shell…

Suddenly, Brutus heard a noise, someone knocking on his door. He looked up, but the sky was full of storm clouds blotting out the stars and he couldn't tell how soon it would be day. It was certainly too late, or too early, for visitors.

'Lucius!' he said, calling out to his servant. 'Go and see who that is.'

The servant scurried off to do his master's bidding, and Brutus went back to his dark thoughts, brooding on what he knew had to be done, uneasy with his decision. It felt as if his mind was at war with itself, and he was trapped in a strange dream. But he was determined to carry this through.

Just then Lucius returned. 'It's your friend

Cassius, sir,' he said. 'There are others with him, but I don't know who they are. They've all half-covered their faces with their cloaks.'

'So, the plotters have arrived,' said Brutus. 'They must be very nervous if they feel the need to disguise themselves even at night... Let them in, Lucius.'

A few moments later Lucius showed the men inside, and they uncovered their faces. Brutus knew Cassius, of course, and Casca, and he recognised the others, too – Decius and Cinna, Metellus and Trebonius, all members of the Senate.

'We're sorry to trouble you at this time of night, Brutus,' said Cassius. The others looked on, saying nothing. 'Can you and I talk privately for a moment?'

'Of course,' said Brutus. 'And don't worry, I wasn't in bed.'

Brutus and Cassius went off to a dark corner of the garden and whispered together for a while. Eventually Brutus gave a small nod. He had thrown in his lot with the plotters – Caesar was to die that morning in the Senate, and Brutus would be one of the assassins. He and Cassius soon returned to the others.

'Let us shake hands,' Brutus said solemnly. 'Each man with all the rest.'

'We should swear an oath,' said Cassius. But Brutus shook his head.

'We don't need to, Cassius,' he said. 'We're Romans, and our word should be our bond.' Brutus talked for quite some time, explaining why Cassius had been wrong. Cassius flushed slightly as he waited for Brutus to finish.

'Well then, who else shall we try and persuade to join us?' Cassius said, changing the subject. 'What about Cicero? He would be a real asset.'

Several of the others agreed, especially Casca. Brutus, however, didn't.

'Fine, we'll leave Cicero out, then,' muttered Cassius with a scowl, irritation in his voice. The others hurried to agree with Brutus, Casca included.

'There is something else,' said Decius. 'Will Caesar be the only one to die?'

'Good question, Decius,' said Cassius. 'We should get rid of Mark Antony, too. He's a clever man, and even on his own he could be a real threat to us.'

'I don't think so,' Brutus said firmly. 'Mark Antony is only interested in drinking and parties. Besides, killing him as well as Caesar would be going too far – the people will think we're no more than butchers. All we want is to prevent Caesar from becoming a tyrant, and I wish we could do it without spilling his blood. But as there's no other way, let's at least carve him like a dish fit for the gods, not a piece of meat for the dogs. Then the people will see that our cause is noble – we're getting rid of Caesar for the good of Rome.'

Cassius kept trying to argue for Mark Antony's death, but Brutus would have none of it. A distant owl hooted and Brutus looked up at the night sky again.

'Morning won't be long now,' he said. 'Perhaps it's time we parted…'

'It's too early,' said Cassius. 'Caesar will still be at home, and he may not even go to the Senate today. He has become quite superstitious lately, and the strange things that have happened tonight might already have put him off.'

'Don't worry,' Decius said eagerly. 'I'll go over to his house and persuade him to come. He can never resist a little flattery, and I know just what to say.'

'Good idea,' said Cassius. 'We'll give you some time and meet you there. We'll leave you, Brutus, and let us remember that we are Romans!'

'Yes, and remember to look cheerful, too,' said Brutus. 'We don't want our faces to give away what's truly in our hearts. I bid you all good day, friends. If you see the noble Caius Ligarius, send him to me. He will join us, I'm sure.'

The conspirators left the garden, hurrying out into the dark streets of the city once more. Brutus called for Lucius, but the boy did not appear. 'He must have gone to sleep,' he thought enviously. 'The boy has no cares or worries to keep him awake, like me. No matter, let him enjoy the sweetness of slumber.'

'Brutus, my lord,' said a voice behind him. Brutus was startled from his dark thoughts and turned round. His wife Portia had come into the garden.

'What are you doing outside, Portia?' he said, going over to her. 'You know you shouldn't be in the night air. Why, you'll catch your death of cold.'

'I'm worried about you, Brutus,' said Portia. 'You haven't been sleeping, and then at supper last night you suddenly jumped up and started walking about, muttering and sighing. When I asked you what was wrong, you stared at me as if I wasn't there, and then you grew cross and waved me away. So I left you alone, hoping it was just some passing mood that has stopped you eating, talking, sleeping. But it isn't, is it? Tell me what's making you like this!'

'I haven't been feeling well, that's all,' said Brutus, not meeting her gaze.

'I don't believe it,' said Portia. 'I've seen you ill, and this is different.'

'I promise I'll be fine, Portia,' said Brutus. 'Now please, go back to bed.'

'Not until you tell me the truth,' said Portia. 'You're not sick – something is playing on your mind and upsetting you. Does it have anything to do with those men who came to see you tonight? There were six or seven of them, and I saw that they had hidden their faces. You shouldn't keep secrets from your wife. Tell me what's going on! Or do our wedding vows mean nothing to you? I won't give anything away, I swear it. You know you can rely on me.'

'You are my wife, as dear to me as life,' said Brutus. 'I wish the gods could make me worthy of you.' Just then there was more knocking on the door. 'Go inside, Portia, quickly now. I'll join you in a while and reveal everything.'

Portia left him reluctantly and soon Lucius – awake once more – brought in yet another man with his face half-covered by his cloak. 'Leave us, boy,' Brutus growled, turning to the man, and Lucius did as he was told. 'Is that you, Caius Ligarius? How are you feeling?' Brutus knew Caius Ligarius had been unwell.

'Yes, it's me, Brutus,' said Caius Ligarius, pulling the cloak away from his face. He coughed and blew his nose. 'And I don't feel great, to be honest.'

'That's a shame,' murmured Brutus. 'This is not a good time to be sick.'

Caius Ligarius gave him a shrewd look. 'I think I could get better if you wanted me to,' he said. 'Does the noble Brutus have a great exploit in mind?'

'I do, my friend,' said Brutus. 'Rome, too, is sick, but we're going to cure it.'

'I have a feeling that means someone is

going to end up feeling quite ill,' said Caius Ligarius. 'No matter – if *you* say it needs to be done, so be it.'

Thunder boomed above them, and lightning flashed, the same lightning that Caesar watched as he stood by a window in his house. The room was large and full of rich furniture. Caesar was in his nightgown, and a slave stood nearby.

'Neither heaven nor earth has been at peace tonight,' Caesar muttered. Even his wife Calpurnia had been restless. She had cried out the same thing three times in her sleep: *Help! Caesar is being murdered!* His nerves were already on edge, and that certainly hadn't helped. There was a huge amount at stake, and Caesar needed some reassurance. 'Tell the priests to make a sacrifice,' he told the slave. 'Then come straight back and report to me what they have to say about my chances of success at the Senate today.'

The Romans believed their priests could work out what the future might bring by sacrificing animals and studying their entrails and internal organs for signs.

'I will, my lord Caesar,' said the slave, and ran off just as Calpurnia came in.

'Are you staying at home today, husband?' she asked. She was in her nightgown, too, and her face was deathly pale and drawn. 'I think you should.'

'Caesar will go out!' he growled, proudly squaring his shoulders and raising his chin. 'Caesar has always faced his enemies, not hidden from them.'

'Please, Caesar,' said Calpurnia. 'I'm not usually superstitious, but the strange things that have happened tonight have frightened me – they say that graves split open and the dead walked, and that fiery warriors fought in the clouds.'

'I refuse to worry,' said Caesar, turning to look out at the darkened city again. 'The Gods have determined all our fates, so there's nothing I can do about mine. Death comes when it will.

Besides, these omens might have nothing to do with me – they could be meant for anyone.'

'But it's only when beggars die that no marvels are seen,' said Calpurnia, tears in her eyes. 'Heaven itself blazes out for the death of a great man!'

'Calm yourself, my love,' said Caesar, smiling. 'It never pays to be afraid. Cowards die in their minds many times over before death actually takes them. The brave die only once...' Just then the slave hurried back into the room and knelt before his master. 'Well, what do the priests say?' Caesar asked.

'They advise you to stay at home today, Caesar,' said the slave. 'The signs aren't good. They killed a beast and cut it open, but could not find a heart.'

Caesar frowned and paced up and down the room, wondering what to do. The truth was that he felt unsettled, too, despite what he had just said to his wife. Perhaps it would be best to stay at home... But he was half-convinced that the sacrifice meant the gods were telling him he should go to the Senate, or be thought a coward, a man without a heart. At last he made up his mind. 'I'll stay at home, Calpurnia,' he said. 'More for your sake than mine, of course.'

Just then Decius arrived, another slave ushering him into Caesar's presence. 'Hail, Caesar!' said Decius. 'I've come to take you to the Senate house.'

'I'm glad you're here, Decius,' said Caesar. 'You can pass on my good wishes to the senators, and tell them I'm not coming today.'

'But why, Caesar?' said Decius. 'Everyone will be so disappointed!'

'Calpurnia had a bad dream,' said Caesar. 'She saw a statue of me spouting blood like a fountain, and people washing their hands in it. She thinks it means something evil is going to happen, and she wants me to stay at home.'

'I don't think that's the right way to interpret such a dream,' said Decius. 'In fact, I think it probably means the opposite! It's telling you that Rome will be revived after all its troubles by feeding on your strength and greatness.'

'Do you really?' said Caesar. 'Umm, I think you might have a point.'

'And I'll tell you something else, Caesar,' said Decius. 'The Senate has decided to make you our king today, but they might change their minds if you don't come. Perhaps they'll say you listen to your wife too much...'

'That settles it!' Caesar muttered crossly. 'Slave, fetch my toga! Your dreams and fears are foolish, Calpurnia. I am ashamed I listened to them. Caesar *will* go to the Senate, and look, here are some friends to accompany me!'

Brutus and the other conspirators had arrived, and Mark Antony, too.

'Noble Caesar, the morning is upon us,' said Brutus, smiling. 'It is time to leave.'

Soon Caesar set off, thinking this was the most important day of his life. And beside him walked Brutus, one hand inside his toga, holding a knife.

Act Three
Murder and Mischief

The usual noisy crowd was waiting outside the Senate when Caesar and the others came into view. There were the Senators, of course, standing in groups, laughing and talking as they waited for the day's session to begin, their togas as white as snow in the spring sunshine. Milling around them were people seeking favours, or those who had grievances they wanted raised in the Senate.

Caesar led the way up the steps to the front of the Senate house with its tall columns and great bronze doors beyond them. The crowd cheered wildly, parting before him like the sea when some monster of the deep cuts through the waves. Then he spotted the soothsayer from the day before, and stopped.

'Well, the Ides of March has come, old man,' Caesar said to him, and turned to Mark Antony, grinning and winking.

Mark Antony grinned back at him.

'Aye, it has, Caesar,' muttered the soothsayer. 'But it's not yet gone.'

Caesar tutted, his grin instantly becoming a scowl. He turned on his heel and stomped off up the steps, then through the doors and into the Senate's main chamber, an immense room with rows of banked seating in circles around a large open space, the walls lined with statues of famous Romans. Most of the Senators had followed Caesar in, and soon he was surrounded by men in togas clamouring for his attention or trying to give him documents, letters, petitions.

'Please, gentlemen, one at a time!' Mark Antony yelled.

Brutus and Cassius and the other conspirators were pushed to one side. They stood watching, their faces anxious, wondering what was being said to Caesar.

'I'm worried about Popilius Lena,' hissed Cassius. 'I think he knows what we're up to and is going to warn Caesar... Look, he's talking to him now.'

'Relax, Cassius,' said Brutus, not taking his eyes off Caesar and the scrum of senators around him. 'Popilius is smiling, and Caesar doesn't seem worried.'

'You're right,' said Cassius, relieved. 'It will be fine, I'm sure it will.'

Their plan was simple, and now they put it into action, the conspirators quickly pushing through the crowd. One of them, Trebonius, talked to Mark Antony and drew him away while the rest gathered near Caesar. Metellus kept him occupied with a lengthy plea, loudly asking Caesar to pardon his brother Publius, whom Caesar had ordered into exile over some trivial matter. Caesar listened impatiently, while Casca quietly moved into position behind him.

'Give up, Metellus,' said Caesar at last. 'It's no good begging. Caesar is like the north star that always holds its place in the sky, and will not yield.'

'You will yield to us now, tyrant!' Casca shouted. He pulled out the hidden knife from inside the folds of his toga – and stabbed Caesar in the back.

Caesar staggered, his face a mask of shock and horror, but there was no escape. Now all the plotters pulled out their knives and fell on him like wolves attacking a deer. The blades rose up and down, slicing into Caesar, his blood spraying across their white togas and splattering onto the marble floor. He tried to fight back, punching out with his fists and roaring. But then he saw Brutus and his courage seemed to drain from him. He had always thought of Brutus as a friend, and here he was with rest of them, a bloodied knife in his hand.

'Even you, Brutus?' Caesar whispered, and slowly sank to the floor near the base of one of the statues. He pulled a fold of his toga over his head, and lay quite still as the assassins finished him off in a frenzy of stabbing and kicking.

'Liberty! Freedom is restored!' yelled the conspirators, holding their knives up in triumph. 'The tyrant is dead! Long live the Republic and the Senate!'

The Senate, however, was in total uproar,

the chamber emptying rapidly as most of the senators fled for their lives. Some stood their ground and yelled 'Shame!' and 'Murderers!' at the conspirators. Brutus dropped his knife and held out his hands to them, Caesar's blood still dripping from his fingers.

'Stop, don't be frightened!' he shouted. 'This ends with Caesar's death...'

But the remaining senators refused to listen and followed the rest out. There were distant screams in the streets, although suddenly an eerie hush filled the chamber. The conspirators stood staring down at Caesar's body, a dark pool of blood spreading from it across the marble floor and staining their sandals.

'Well, what now?' said Cinna. They were all panting, their eyes wild.

'We must all stand fast together,' said Metellus. 'In case one of Caesar's – '

'Look, here comes Trebonius,' said Cassius. 'Where is Mark Antony?'

'He has fled to his house, stunned by what

has happened,' said Trebonius. 'The people are shocked, too – it's as if they think it's the end of the world.'

'It's the end of Caesar's world, anyway,' said Brutus. 'We should go to the Forum, raise our bloodied weapons and proclaim that as loudly as we can!'

'We're heroes!' said Cassius, his eyes gleaming. 'Why, men will act out this scene hundreds of years from now in places we've never even heard of.'

'I'm sure you're right, Cassius,' said Brutus. 'And they'll say Caesar ended his days at the feet of great Pompey after all – this is Pompey's statue.'

The conspirators looked up at the blank face of the statue, all of them feeling uneasy at such irony. But then Brutus heard a noise and turned round. A slave had entered the chamber. He approached Brutus and kneeled before him.

'My master Mark Antony sent me, my lord,' said the slave, his head bowed. 'He told me to say he thought you were wise, noble, brave and honest. And that he would like to come and speak with you, if you give him safe passage.'

'Your master is wise and brave, too,' said Brutus. 'We would be happy to speak with him. He can come here, and be sure that he will leave untouched.'

'Thank you, my lord, I'll fetch him now,' said the slave, and hurried off.

'There, do you see?' Brutus said triumphantly, turning to the others. 'Mark Antony doesn't want to be our enemy. I knew he'd come round to our way!'

'I only hope you're right,' Cassius muttered darkly. 'I still don't trust him...'

'Sssh! Here he comes now,' hissed Brutus. 'Welcome, Mark Antony.'

Mark Antony walked slowly across the chamber and stopped by Caesar's body. 'Mighty Caesar,' he murmured, his voice almost breaking, his face pale, his eyes rimmed with red. 'Have you fallen so low? Are all your triumphs reduced to this?' He looked at the plotters. 'I don't know what your intentions are, gentlemen,' he said. 'But if you want to kill me, this is the best moment to do it. With great Caesar gone, I'll never be so ready to die as I am now.'

'We don't want to kill you, Antony,' said Brutus, his voice soft. 'I know you probably think we're bloody and cruel, but we only did this because our hearts were full of pity – pity for Rome. We have always thought of you as a friend.'

'Yes, you could even have a say in who gets the best jobs,' said Cassius. 'Everything will be up for grabs now, Antony, and we've got the advantage.'

'But first we have to calm the people,' said Brutus, scowling at Cassius as if he thought his fellow plotter had gone too far. 'Then I'll explain to you exactly why someone like me felt forced to do this deed. You know I loved Caesar.'

'I have no doubt you acted from the best motives, Brutus,' said Mark Antony. 'Let me shake your hands, all of you.'

Each of the plotters shook Antony by the hand, their faces solemn.

'Perhaps you think I'm a coward,' he murmured at last. 'And if your spirit is looking down on me, Caesar, how angry you must be to see me shaking their hands with your blood on their fingers. Forgive me, great Julius. You're like a noble stag that has been struck down by hunters...'

He turned to look at Caesar's corpse again, tears flowing down his cheeks.

Cassius took his arm and said, 'Mark Antony – ' but Antony shook him off.

'I'll thank you not to interrupt my grieving, Cassius,' he snarled.

'I'm not trying to,' said Cassius, stepping back. 'I'd just like to be clear about your intentions. Are you really with us now? Can we count on your support?'

'Did I say you couldn't?' said Antony. 'I shook your hands in friendship. And if it's all the same to you, I would like to speak at Caesar's funeral.'

'Of course you can,' said Brutus. Now it was Cassius's turn to scowl.

'What in Jupiter's name are you doing, Brutus?' he whispered, pulling Brutus aside. 'We can't let him do that. He might try to turn the people against us.'

'I don't think so,' Brutus hissed back, annoyed. 'It will look better for us if we make sure Caesar has a proper funeral, and Antony should be part of it. But don't worry, I'll speak first and explain to the people why we killed Caesar. And before Antony speaks I'll tell them he's only there with *our* permission.'

'But who knows what mischief he'll get up to?' said Cassius. 'I don't like it.'

Cassius, however, had no say in the matter. Brutus had already turned his attention back to Mark Antony. 'Good, so that's settled,' he said, smiling. 'Just make sure you don't say anything bad about us,' he added.

'Fear not, Brutus,' said Mark Antony. 'Nothing is further from my mind.'

Brutus led the assassins out, leaving Mark Antony alone with Caesar's body. Antony watched them go, outwardly calm. But inside he was seething with fury.

'I curse these men, and I swear they will pay for this foul crime,' he growled. 'Caesar, your spirit will return with the lord of Hell, unleashing the dogs of war and bringing havoc to Rome!'

Just then a slave came into the chamber and approached him. 'You're Octavius Caesar's man, aren't you?' said Antony.

Young Octavius was Caesar's great-nephew and heir, and Antony knew that Caesar had summoned him to Rome. 'I am, my lord,' said the slave. 'He sent me to tell you that he isn't far from the city ... but oh, gods! Poor Caesar...'

The slave had seen Caesar's body, and was

horrified. Antony thought of sending the slave straight back to Octavius to tell him what had happened, and warn him to stay clear of Rome for the time being. But it might be wiser to wait until after he had made his speech at Caesar's funeral. Then he would have a much better idea of how the people felt, and what he and Octavius should do.

'I'll explain everything later,' said Antony. 'In the meantime, you'd better come with me. I have to arrange for Caesar's body to be taken to the Forum...'

Mark Antony hurried out of the chamber now, too, heading for his house, where he had armed men to protect him. Things were tense on the streets of Rome. The news had spread like wildfire, and soon angry crowds stood on corners, some talking in hushed voices, others shouting, all of them hardly able to believe that Caesar had been murdered. Word went round that Caesar's body was being taken to the Forum, and that Brutus and Mark Antony were going to speak. By mid-afternoon it seemed that everyone in Rome was there.

Brutus stood at the top of the steps of the Temple of Jupiter to address the huge crowd. Caesar's body was laid out on a bier just below him, and legionaries in battle gear stood on either side, low sunlight glinting off their armour and shields, the red crests of their helmets like splashes of blood.

'My fellow Romans,' Brutus began. 'You know me as a man of honour...'

He spoke for quite some time, explaining that he and the others had killed Caesar because they loved their country, and that he would kill himself then and there if anyone thought he had done it for another reason. There was some heckling, but not that much, and it seemed that Brutus had them on his side.

'And now the noble Mark Antony, Caesar's friend, would like to speak,' he said at last. 'Although I would add that he only does so with our permission. Anyway, I would urge all of you not to leave until you have heard what he has to say.'

Brutus gestured for Mark Antony to step forward, and then left. Antony stood at the top of the steps as Brutus had done, and remained silent for a moment, looking down on the crowd below him. 'Friends, Romans and countrymen,' he said at last. 'Lend me your ears... I come to bury Caesar, not to praise him.' But he did praise him, reminding the Roman people of everything that Caesar had done – the nations he had conquered for them, the treasure he had brought back to fill the empire's coffers, the glory he had brought to Rome's name.

The crowd cheered Caesar's memory, but they fell silent again when Antony talked of the conspirators, and how Brutus had claimed that Caesar was too ambitious. 'Brutus is an honourable man,' said Antony. 'But you all know I offered Caesar a crown three times, and three times he turned it down.'

The crowd murmured angrily, and Antony

worked on them, whipping up their fury against the murderers. Soon the crowd was yelling, calling out for their deaths.

Antony's face lit up with a grin. Now let the mischief truly begin...

ACT FOUR
ARMIES ON THE MARCH

The streets of Rome were filled once more with restless crowds, although perhaps mobs would be a better word. Until Antony's funeral speech, the people had been frightened by what had happened, uncertain what to believe or who to support. But Antony had made things easy. Now they were sure Caesar had been a hero, and that the plotters should pay dearly for what they'd done.

The mobs knew where Brutus and Cassius and the others lived, and by the evening their houses were burning, the flames lighting the sky over the city. Most of the plotters managed to escape, fleeing with little more than the clothes they wore, but some were caught and torn limb from limb. One man – the poet Cinna – was unlucky enough to die because he had the same name as a plotter.

Mark Antony stood at the window of his grand villa watching the blood-red sky. Lying on couches behind him were Octavius and Lepidus, a man older than the other two, and much richer as well. Lepidus wore a toga, but Antony had changed into his military uniform, his breastplate reflecting the distant fires, his short sword – the *gladius* of the legions – in a scabbard at his side. Octavius was in uniform, too, but he was still covered in the dust and dirt of his journey.

Antony turned and walked over to a low table. A heap of papyrus rolls stood on it, each one covered with a long list of names. None of the three men had enough supporters to claim power alone now Caesar was gone, so they had decided to join forces. They had begun by working out who they could count on and, more importantly, who would be against them. 'These then shall die,' said Antony, picking up one of the rolls. 'Their names are all marked.'

'Your brother, too, Lepidus,' said Octavius. Caesar's heir was very young, barely a grown man, and quite slender. But he had a strong face with a faint resemblance to Caesar, and an air of certainty about him. 'Do you agree?'

Lepidus shrugged. 'So long as Antony's nephew Publius dies, too.'

'That's all right by me,' said Antony. 'Look, I've damned him with a cross against his name. Listen, Lepidus, I think you should go to Caesar's house and dig out a copy of his will. We need to look at it and make sure we don't give away too much of his fortune in legacies, whatever he might have wanted...'

Octavius smiled to himself. He knew Mark Antony had made a great show of telling the people at Caesar's funeral how generous Caesar had been in his will, and that many would benefit from it. But that had just been to keep the fools in the streets on their side. He and Antony weren't stupid enough to give away Caesar's money when they needed all they could get to pay for the coming war.

'Er, good idea!' said Lepidus, hurrying off.

Antony scowled after him. 'The man's a moron, only fit to be sent on errands,' he muttered. 'It seems madness to divide up the world and give someone like him a third of it!'

'If that's what you think, why did you let him add names to the lists of who should die?' Octavius said. His voice was soft, but his eyes were hard.

'Trust me on this, Octavius,' said Antony. 'I'm older than you, so I know what I'm doing. We'll use Lepidus to do our dirty work for the time being, and then as soon as he's no longer useful, we'll cut him loose. But we have more important things to discuss. Brutus and Cassius are putting together an army – we need to do the same as soon as possible, and to make some plans.'

'Quite right,' said Octavius, jumping to his feet. 'This is a dangerous time, and we have many enemies. Even some of our allies might be false friends.'

Things moved quickly over the next few weeks. Brutus and Cassius had crossed the Adriatic Sea to Illyria, and most of the legions in the eastern part of the Empire joined them. But Mark Antony and Octavius raised an army from Caesar's old legions in Italy and the other western provinces. And soon both armies were marching down the long, straight Roman roads, seeking out each other like two red-crested, many-legged monsters of sharp steel and soft flesh.

Brutus and Cassius split up at one point, Cassius going off to recruit more troops, Brutus setting up a fortified camp near the coast. As was their habit, the legionaries dug a deep ditch around the camp and used the soil to build a square rampart, adding a wall of sharpened stakes on top. Then they put up their tents in straight rows, with a large tent for Brutus and his officers in the centre.

It was a warm summer's day when Cassius returned, his new recruits behind him on the road. A messenger rode ahead to let Brutus know Cassius was coming, a certain Lucilius, a man who had served Brutus for many years.

'Well then, Lucilius,' said Brutus, emerging from his tent. The two soldiers guarding it, one on either side of the flap, snapped to attention. Brutus was in full armour, sunshine glinting off his breastplate. 'Is Cassius near at last?'

'He is, and sends you his greetings,' said Lucilius, jumping off his horse.

'A word with you, Lucilius,' Brutus said quietly, drawing the messenger away from the guards. 'Now tell me honestly, how did Cassius treat you?'

'Well enough,' said Lucilius. 'But he wasn't as friendly as he used to be.'

'Ah, I thought so,' said Brutus. 'His feelings towards me are cooling.'

Just then they heard the sound of horses and men marching, their armour and weapons chinking. Cassius rode up and dismounted, his recruits behind him.

'I bid you welcome, Cassius!' said Brutus, raising a hand in greeting.

'Most noble brother, you have done me

wrong!' Cassius shouted. He stamped right up to Brutus and stood before him, a scowl on his beaky Roman face.

'But I don't understand...' murmured Brutus, confused. Cassius opened his mouth to say something else, but Brutus stopped him before he could get going. 'Keep your voice down,' he whispered. 'We really shouldn't argue in front of the men. Come into my tent and tell me what's upset you so much.'

Cassius agreed to do as Brutus asked, but it was clear he was very angry. The tent was plainly furnished – it contained a couch for Brutus to sleep on, a chest for his clothes, a stand for his armour, a table covered in lists and maps. The two men stood facing each other. 'You condemned one of my men, Lucius Pella, for supposedly taking bribes,' Cassius snarled. 'And then you simply chose to ignore my letter to you saying that you should let him off.'

'You should never have written it,' snapped Brutus. 'He was guilty and that's all there is to it. But then it seems you've been taking a few bribes yourself.'

'How ... how dare you!' spluttered Cassius, his face red. 'If anyone else had accused me of such a thing, those would be the last words they ever spoke!'

'You should be ashamed of yourself,' said Brutus. 'Don't you remember why we acted as we did on the Ides of March? We killed Caesar for the sake of a just cause, for the good of Rome. Are we going to contaminate ourselves now with bribes? I'd rather be a dog and howl at the moon than be a wretch like that.'

'Take care, Brutus!' Cassius yelled in the other man's face, spit flying from his lips. 'You don't want to make me do something I'll regret, do you?'

'You've already done things you should be sorry for, Cassius,' hissed Brutus, not giving any ground. 'And you don't frighten me, however much you yell. It's all a lot of hot air. And what about that gold I asked you for?

Unlike you, I'm not willing to extract money from the local peasants by force, but I still have to pay my legions. I wrote to you for help, and you turned me down!'

They wrangled on, shouting and yelling, giving vent to their frustration and worries, until finally Cassius sank onto the couch in despair. 'I wish Antony and Octavius were here to take their revenge on me now,' he moaned, holding his head in his hands. 'I'm tired of this world, of being told what to do and having my faults thrown in my face.' He pulled a dagger from a scabbard on his belt and held the hilt out to Brutus. 'Kill me as you did Caesar,' he moaned. 'For even when you hated him, you loved him better than you have loved me...'

'Put your dagger away, Cassius,' said Brutus, shaking his head and sighing. 'Your anger always goes as quickly as it comes. I was wrong to argue, too.'

Cassius stood up and they hugged, slapping each other's backs. One of the guards looked in through the flap and nervously asked if they were all right.

'We're fine,' Brutus said. 'Have some wine brought in, and ask Messala to come and see us, will you?' The guard nodded and let the tent flap fall again. But now it was Brutus' turn to sit on the couch, his head in his hands. 'Oh, Cassius, I am sick with grief,' he murmured. 'My wife Portia is dead.'

'I'm sorry to hear such bad news,' said Cassius. 'Had she been ill?'

'No, I left her alone in Rome, and the growing power of Octavius and Mark Antony frightened her,' said Brutus. 'She lost her mind … and killed herself.'

Cassius put a hand on his friend's shoulder, and just then Brutus' servant Lucius came in with a jug of wine, and Messala behind him. Messala was a grizzled old soldier, and chief of staff to the army of the plotters. Lucius poured wine into cups for the three men, then Brutus asked the servant to leave them.

'Our intelligence reports tell me our enemies are making for the town of Philippi, Messala,' said Brutus. 'Is that right? It isn't very far from here.'

'That seems to be their plan,' growled Messala. 'We've also heard that Octavius and Antony have had a hundred senators put to death in Rome.'

'As many as that?' said Brutus. 'I'd heard it was only seventy, including Cicero... Anyway, I think we should march on Philippi and confront them.'

'Oh no, I don't agree,' said Cassius, horrified. 'We should let our enemies tire themselves out trying to find us, while we keep rested and stay nimble.'

Brutus shook his head once more, over-ruling him. 'Their army is still growing, and ours won't get any bigger. Besides, we're ready to fight now. If you leap into the flood when the tide is going your way, it will take you to glory. But if you miss that moment, all that happens is you drown.'

As usual, Cassius gave in, defeated by Brutus' firmness and eloquence, and it was decided that the army should set off at first light. Night had already fallen, and now Cassius and Messala shook hands with Brutus and left. Brutus made ready to sleep, asking Lucius to sing him a song to calm his racing mind.

Lucius sat at the end of the couch, playing his lyre and singing in a quiet voice. But he fell asleep first. Brutus smiled, then picked up a roll of papyrus and started reading. After a while, he looked up – and his blood ran cold.

The ghost of Caesar was standing over him, its bloody wounds gaping.

'Why … why have you come?' whispered Brutus, his heart thumping.

'To tell you that you'll see me at Philippi,' the ghost murmured, its face unforgiving. Brutus opened his mouth to say something else, but it was too late. The ghost vanished, the tent flapping wildly as if there were a storm outside.

Brutus shook his head, trying to get the image out of his mind.

But it haunted his dreams, and no rest could he find.

74

Act Five
The Noblest Roman

The rival armies found each other at last, near the town of Philippi in Illyria. Both sides took up position, the morning sun glinting off weapons and armour, the dusty air full of the sounds of soldiers shouting and horses neighing. But no one crossed the open ground between the armies as yet. Now was the time to organise and prepare for the coming battle, and to observe the enemy, too.

Octavius and Antony were in the centre of their line, sitting astride their horses, their officers flanking them, scanning the troops opposite. 'Well, it looks like you were wrong, Antony,' said Octavius, the tall red crest on his shiny helmet rippling in the light breeze. 'You thought they wouldn't be willing to face us and would stay in the hills. But here they are, ready to take us on, it seems.'

'They're trying to show us they're not scared,' said Antony. 'But if you ask me, they'd rather be anywhere else. You will advance on the left, Octavius –'

'Oh no, my men will advance on the right,' Octavius said firmly, and Antony glared at him, obviously quite cross at being contradicted. The two allies were just beginning to argue with each other properly when a messenger rode up.

'Small party approaching on horseback under a flag of truce, sir!' he said, saluting Octavius. 'It's Brutus and Cassius, and I think they want to talk.'

Octavius and Mark Antony rode out of the line with a few guards to protect them. Brutus and Cassius, who had also brought their own guards along, were waiting in the open ground halfway between the two armies.

'I thought it would be a good idea to talk a little before we come to blows, my fellow countrymen,' said Brutus. 'Perhaps we could settle our differences...'

'I don't think so,' said Octavius. 'We're not so fond of talking as you.'

'Lying, more like,' growled Antony, moving his horse forward. 'Aren't you the men who walked up to Caesar crying "Hail, Caesar! Long live Caesar!" and then stabbed him to death? You're nothing but a bunch of murderers.

You two were practically kissing his feet while that dog Casca crept up behind him.'

'Be careful what you say, Antony,' hissed Cassius. He nudged his horse forward, too, and now the two Roman nobles glared at each other, their faces inches apart. 'If I'd had my way, you wouldn't be alive to talk to us at all.'

'Shall we get to the point?' said Octavius. He suddenly drew his sword and held it high. The guards with Brutus and Cassius drew their swords, too, and one of them quickly rode forward, pushing between Cassius and Mark Antony. Octavius, however, sat motionless in his saddle, his face stern. 'I swear my sword will not rest until Caesar has been revenged,' he said. 'Or I am dead.'

'I'd be happy to oblige you, young man,' said Brutus, scowling. 'And don't forget, being killed by the noble Brutus would be quite an honour.'

'Really?' said Octavius. 'I don't think I was born to die on your sword.'

'Being killed by Brutus is too good for you,' said Cassius. 'You're nothing but a bad-tempered schoolboy, and your companion is a drunk and a loser.'

'Just watch your mouth, Cassius!' yelled Antony, drawing his own sword. There was a lot of yelling and swearing and jostling and horses neighing. But then Octavius grabbed the bridle of Antony's horse and pulled him away.

'We hurl defiance in your teeth, traitors!' he called out, his voice ringing clear. 'Let's get this battle started – if you have the courage to fight us, that is!'

With that, both groups rode back to their own lines. Orders were given, the great Roman battle trumpets were blown, and the front ranks moved forward, the rhythmic thumping of their iron-shod sandals making the ground shake.

Cassius wheeled his horse round behind the lines of advancing soldiers, and found himself beside Messala. The grizzled veteran sat rigidly on his horse, his dark eyes narrowed beneath the iron rim of his helmet. 'Now comes the storm of steel, and everything depends on our luck in what happens next,' Cassius murmured, watching Brutus ride over to speak to one of the other officers.

'I'm sorry, Cassius?' said Messala, turning to him. 'What did you say?'

'And it's my birthday today,' said Cassius, lost in thought, his voice quiet. He pulled himself together. 'Listen, Messala, I want you to be my witness,' he said, taking the other man's hand. 'I was against staking everything on just this one battle – I think it's a grave mistake. I never used to be superstitious, but have you noticed the sky above us is full of ravens and crows waiting for us to die?'

'Surely things aren't that bad,' said Messala, trying to reassure him, but Cassius refused to be cheered up.

After a while, Brutus rode over to them. More orders were given, and Brutus sent Messala off with some new instructions, leaving the two allies to talk. Cassius was still in a sombre mood.

'I hope things go well today, Brutus,' he said at last. 'But this could be the last time we speak to each other, so we should think about the worst that might happen. What are your plans if we lose? You know Octavius and Mark Antony will drag you in chains through the streets of Rome if they capture you.'

'I won't let them, Cassius,' said Brutus, smiling and shaking his head. 'I will never go bound to Rome – I'm too good for that. Today we will end the journey that we began on the Ides of March, and I have no idea whether you and I will see each other again. So let's say goodbye now. If we do meet again, why then we'll smile. But if we don't, then we can say that this was the best way to part.'

'Farewell then, Brutus,' said Cassius, and the two friends shook hands.

'Lead on, Cassius,' said Brutus. 'If only we could already know how this day will turn out.

But it will certainly end one way or another...
And now, to battle!'

At that moment the two front lines came together with a great CRASH! of steel on steel. Swords rose and fell, men and horses screamed and died, and blood covered the dusty ground. Brutus had spotted that Octavius' troops seemed raw and untested, and had ordered his men to hit them as hard as they could. His tactics soon paid off, and Octavius was forced to give ground.

Cassius, however, was not having quite so much success. His troops met fierce resistance from Antony's legions, which were packed with veterans of Caesar's wars – all of them tough men with a deep grudge against the plotters. Soon Cassius and his men were being pushed back, and then the line broke. Panic-stricken soldiers threw away their weapons and shields and ran to the hills. Cassius tried to stop them, and even cut one of them down himself. An officer on his staff – a certain Titinius – found him standing over the body.

'I had to do it, Titinius,' he groaned. 'The cowards have let me down!'

'It was all Brutus' fault,' said Titinius. 'He gave the order to advance too early. That split our forces and allowed Antony's legions to encircle us.'

Suddenly another man appeared – Pindarus, a slave who belonged to Cassius. 'Run, my lord!' he yelled. 'Mark Antony's men have captured our camp!'

Cassius and Titinius peered into the distance and saw a column of smoke and flame rising from their tents. Cassius could see another column of troops, too.

'Titinius, ride over there and see whether they're friends or enemies,' he said. Titinius nodded, jumped onto his horse, and galloped off. 'Pindarus, go a little further up the slope and watch him. Tell me what you see.'

Pindarus squinted into the sun, a hand sheltering his eyes. 'Titinius has been surrounded by horsemen, my lord,' he said. 'I think they've captured him!'

Cassius sighed, his shoulders slumping. 'Come down again, Pindarus,' he called out. The slave did as he was told, and soon he was standing in front of his master, a puzzled expression on his face. 'I saved your life when I captured you,' said Cassius. 'And in return I made you swear you would do whatever I told you to. Now it's time for you to keep your oath.' Cassius drew out his dagger and pressed the hilt into the slave's hand. 'I want you to kill me.'

Pindarus looked into his master's eyes for a moment. Then Cassius turned his face away and Pindarus drove the dagger into him. Cassius staggered, then fell to the ground, his life's blood pumping out. 'So, now you are revenged on me, Caesar,' Cassius moaned. 'And with the very dagger that helped to kill you...'

Pindarus threw down the blade and ran. But not long after, Titinius rode up, with Messala beside him. The two men jumped from their horses.

'Cassius is no more,' groaned Titinius, looking down at the blood-soaked corpse. 'Our day is done ... he must have thought that I had been captured.'

'I'd better go and tell Brutus,' said Messala. He climbed back into the saddle and galloped off, but Titinius was kneeling by Cassius now, and took no notice.

'I met our friends, Cassius!' moaned Titinius. 'We were coming to meet you, but now we're finished, and I can stand it no more.' He picked up the weapon from beside Cassius's body. 'I'll plunge this dagger into my own heart...'

Messala came thundering back with Brutus and several other officers, but it was too late. Titinius lay dead, his body across that of Cassius. 'Oh, Julius Caesar, you are still mighty!' said Brutus, looking down at the two bodies, his horse restless beneath him. 'Your spirit must be haunting us, making us take our own lives. Are there two Romans as great as these who lie before us?'

'Come, sir, we must get back to the battle,' said one of his officers.

'Yes, you're right,' said Brutus. 'I don't have time to mourn you now, friend Cassius, but I will, I promise.' He wheeled his horse around and held up his sword, the steel blade glinting in the afternoon sun. 'Follow me, men!' he roared. 'The day is not over yet, not by any means. We can still win this!'

But Brutus was wrong. His men were outnumbered now, Antony's legions having come over from their flank to support those of Octavius. Soon Brutus's men were being pushed back across the battlefield, men dying with every bloody backward step, until finally Brutus's legions broke, too. They ran, and were hunted down in the ghastly red twilight, like rabbits fleeing from hunters.

Brutus fled on foot like the rest, his horse having been killed. Only a few men were with him now – Dardanius, Clitus, Volumnius, Strato – and they hurried into the hills, keeping to the shadows, looking for somewhere to hide. Brutus, however, knew there was no escape. 'Let's rest here, by this rock,' he said at last, and the fugitives huddled in the shadows, grateful for some rest.

But Brutus had a rather longer rest on his mind – one that would last forever. He quietly asked Dardanius and Clitus if they would help him to die, but they were horrified and refused. So then he turned to Volumnius.

'You know, I saw the ghost of Caesar last night,' he said. 'I should have known then that we were going to lose. The hour of my death has come.'

'That's not true, my lord,' said Volumnius, tears on his battle-stained cheeks.

'Oh, but I'm sure it is, Volumnius,' said Brutus. Trumpets sounded in the distance, and they could hear the men hunting them calling to each other. 'Our enemies have pushed me to the edge of the grave,' Brutus murmured. 'And it would be far better if I leap myself rather than wait for them to push me in.'

'I just can't do it, my lord,' said Volumnius. 'It's not a job for a friend.'

'Quick, run, my lord!' Clitus hissed suddenly. 'They're almost upon us!'

'You go,' said Brutus. 'Don't worry, I will follow you in a moment.'

Dardanius, Clitus and Volumnius ran off, but Brutus stayed where he was, and held Strato's arm. 'Stay with me, Strato,' he said. 'You're a good man, an honourable man. Will you hold my sword for me so that I can run on to it?'

'Very well,' said Strato. 'But give me your hand first.' Brutus did as he asked, and then handed Strato his sword. Strato held the blade straight out in front of him. 'Farewell, my lord,' he said, turning his face away.

Brutus threw himself forward, gripping Strato's wrist to guide the sword into his own body. 'Farewell, good Strato,' he moaned, and sank to the ground, his hands round the bloody blade. 'I hope you're satisfied now, Caesar,' he said as his eyes glazed over. 'I'm killing myself far more willingly than I killed you...'

Then Brutus died, his last breath leaving him like a sigh of regret. Strato stood beside him, his head bowed, and barely looked up when Octavius and Antony arrived with their men. Messala was with them, having already been pardoned by Octavius, as were all the other surviving members of the plotters' army. Messala walked over to Strato and put an arm round his shoulder.

'Tell me, Strato,' he said, his voice gentle. 'How did Brutus die?'

'I held his sword,' said Strato, almost choked. 'And he ran onto it...'

'This was the noblest Roman of them all,' said Mark Antony, taking off his helmet, the others doing the same. 'The other conspirators were just jealous of Caesar, but Brutus believed he was acting for the good of Rome and its people. He lived a good life, and we could look at him and say – this was a man!'

'We'll give him the burial a man like him truly deserves,' said Octavius. 'We'll put his body in my tent tonight, where he'll lie like a brave soldier.'

So six soldiers raised up his body, took the noble Brutus away.

And a lone Roman trumpet sounded the end of this terrible day.

ABOUT THE AUTHOR

Tony Bradman was born in London and still lives there. He has written a large number of books for children of all ages, including 25 titles about his most popular creation, Dilly the Dinosaur. *Dilly the Dinosaur* was made into a long-running TV series and one of the books was shortlisted for the Children's Book Award. Tony has also edited many anthologies of poetry and short stories.

Tony loves reading about the classical world and Roman history, and also going to see Shakespeare plays performed at the restored Globe Theatre on London's South Bank. So doing an adaptation of Shakespeare's famous play about Julius Caesar was the perfect job!

SHAKESPEARE TODAY

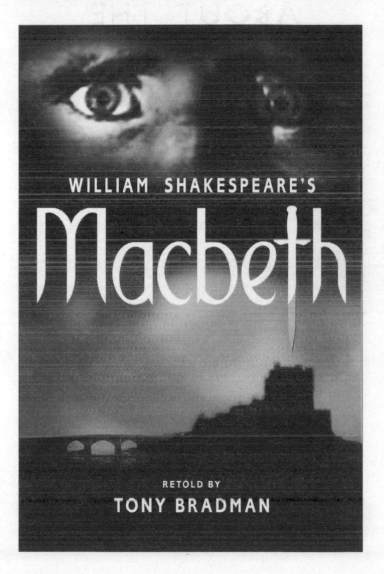

WILLIAM SHAKESPEARE'S

Macbeth

RETOLD BY
TONY BRADMAN

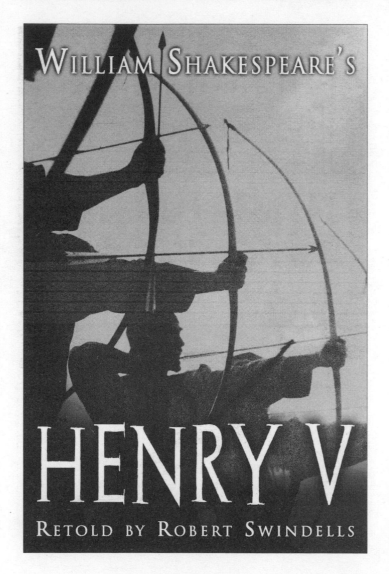

WILLIAM SHAKESPEARE'S

HENRY V

RETOLD BY ROBERT SWINDELLS

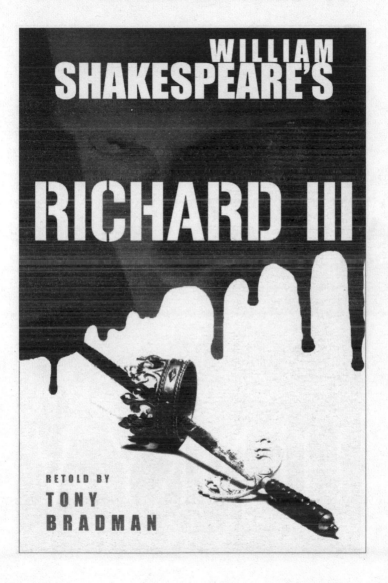

WILLIAM
SHAKESPEARE'S

RICHARD III

RETOLD BY
TONY
BRADMAN

SHAKESPEARE TODAY

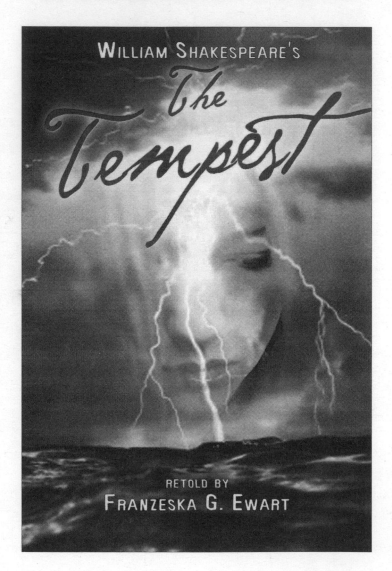

WILLIAM SHAKESPEARE'S

The Tempest

RETOLD BY
FRANZESKA G. EWART